Text copyright © 2023 by Sandra V. Feder
Illustrations copyright © 2023 by Rahele Jomepour Bell

Published in 2023 by Groundwood Books / House of Anansi Press
groundwoodbooks.com

We gratefully acknowledge the Government of Canada for its financial
support of our publishing program.

With the participation of the Government of Canada
Avec la participation du gouvernement du Canada | Canada

Library and Archives Canada Cataloguing in Publication
Title: Peaceful me / words by Sandra V. Feder ; pictures by Rahele
Jomepour Bell.
Names: Feder, Sandra V., author. | Jomepour Bell, Rahele, illustrator.
Identifiers: Canadiana (print) 20220280398 | Canadiana (ebook)
20220280401 | ISBN 9781773063416 (hardcover) |
ISBN 9781773063423 (EPUB) | ISBN 9781773063430 (Kindle)
Classification: LCC PZ7.F334 Pea 2023 | DDC j813/.6—dc23

The illustrations were created with hand-printed textures, which were
scanned and painted digitally.
Design by Michael Solomon and Lucia Kim
Printed and bound in South Korea

In memory of Linda Miller, whose
kindness and love helped me to be a
more peaceful me — SVF

For Eli, who finds peace and carries
it with her wherever she goes — RJB

Peaceful Me

WORDS BY
Sandra V. Feder
PICTURES BY
Rahele Jomepour Bell

Groundwood Books
House of Anansi Press
Toronto / Berkeley

I like feeling peaceful.

Sometimes I feel peaceful when
I'm with other people.

"Free," peaceful.

"Favorite part," peaceful.

Sometimes I feel
peaceful when I'm alone.

"Quiet," peaceful.

Sometimes I feel peaceful when things go well.

"All done," peaceful.

"Good game!" peaceful.

Sometimes I feel peaceful
when I'm with my family.

"Yummy," peaceful.

"Cuddle time," peaceful.

Sometimes I feel peaceful
when I'm outside.

"Fluffy clouds," peaceful.

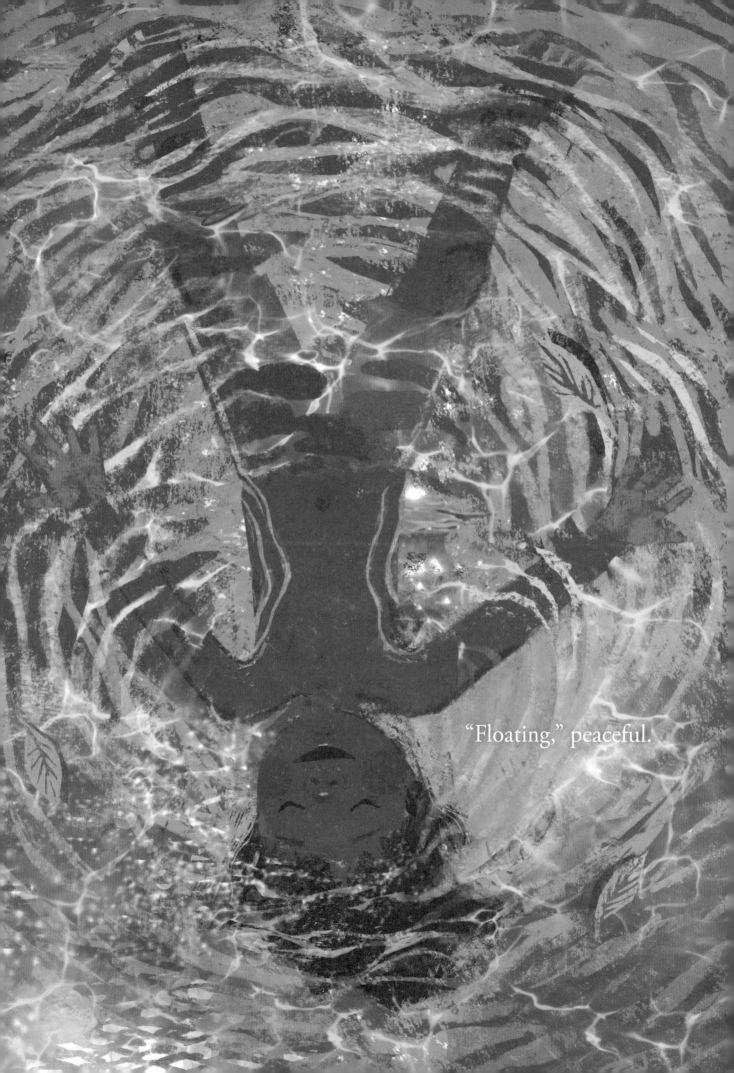

"Floating," peaceful.

Sometimes I feel peaceful when I do something nice.

"For you," peaceful.

"I'll help," peaceful.

Sometimes I feel peaceful
when I'm having fun.

"My turn," peaceful.

"Flying," peaceful.

Sometimes I feel peaceful when I'm not doing anything special.

"Tickling toes," peaceful.

"Aaah," peaceful.

Sometimes I don't feel peaceful.

So I slow my breathing down —
deep breath in, deep breath out.

Sometimes it
helps to picture
something peaceful.

So I imagine my favorite things.

Sometimes it helps
to be in a quiet place.

So I look for one.

Sometimes it
helps to feel a hug.

So I find one.

Sometimes being
peaceful is easy.

Sometimes it takes
work to get there.

But when I do,
I'm happy to be
peaceful me.